Sometimes Smart Is Good

A Veces Es Bueno Ser Listo

Written by
Dena Fox Luchsinger

Paintings by
Karen A. Jerome

Eerdmans Books for Young Readers
Grand Rapids, Michigan • Cambridge, U.K.

Para dos mujeres que me han inspirado
mucho: Beatriz Briones Acosta de Irene
y Paula Leñero de Santos; y por supuesto,
for Andrew

— *D. F. L.*

To my husband, Douglas Bernard Skillins

— *K. A. J.*

Text © 2007 Dena Fox Luchsinger
Illustrations © 2007 Karen A. Jerome
Published in 2007 by Eerdmans Books for Young Readers,
an imprint of Wm. B. Eerdmans Publishing Co.

Wm. B. Eerdmans Publishing Co.
2140 Oak Industrial Dr. N.E., Grand Rapids, Michigan 49505
P.O. Box 163, Cambridge CB3 9PU U.K.

www.eerdmans.com/youngreaders

Manufactured in China

07 08 09 10 11 12   8 7 6 5 4 3 2 1

Library of Congress Cataloging-in-Publication Data

Luchsinger, Dena.
Sometimes smart is good / written by Dena Luchsinger ; illustrated by Karen A. Jerome.
p. cm.
ISBN-13: 978-0-8028-5215-1 (alk. paper)
Summary: While being smart and strong are useful traits, loving other people just because God made them is always good.
[1. Toleration--Fiction. 2. Christian life--Fiction.] I. Jerome, Karen A., ill. II. Title.
PZ7.L96969So 2006
[E]--dc22
2004010239

Translation by Jose Ruiz

Text type set in Redford
Illustrations created with watercolors

Gayle Brown, Art Director
Matthew Van Zomeren, Graphic Designer

Sometimes smart is good . . .

A veces es bueno ser listo . . .

like to help us feel well,
or to create things
that will make life easier,
or to help us understand
our world better.

Como para ayudarnos

a sentirnos bien,

o para hacer cosas

que faciliten la vida,

o para hacer que entendamos

mejor a nuestro mundo.

Sometimes
big and strong is good . . .
like to keep us safe,
or to build important things,
or to help us have fun!

A veces

es bueno ser grande y fuerte . . .

como para mantenernos seguros,

o construir cosas importantes,

¡o para ayudar

a divertirnos!

Sometimes talented is good . . .
like to give us pretty music,
or to help us see the beauty
in the world around us,
or to make us laugh.

A veces es bueno tener talento . . .
como para darnos música bonita,
o para ayudarnos a ver la belleza
del mundo que nos rodea,
o para hacernos reír.

Sometimes.

A veces.

Sometimes we meet people
who don't seem to be smart,
or big and strong,
or talented.

They make us wonder
what is good.

A veces nos encontramos con
personas que no parecen ser listas,
o grandes y fuertes,
o con talento.

Hacen que nos preguntemos
qué es bueno.

What is always good?

Kind is always good . . .
like helping someone,
or visiting a lonely person,
or being a friend.

¿Qué es lo que siempre es bueno?

Siempre es bueno ser amable . . .

como ayudar a alguien,

o visitar a una persona

que se encuentra sola,

o ser un amigo.

Patient is always good . . .
like waiting for a friend to share,
or helping someone to learn,
or giving someone a chance.

Siempre es bueno ser paciente . . .

como esperar a que sea tu turno,

o ayudar a alguien a aprender,

o dar una oportunidad a alguien.

Doing your best is always good . . .
like helping your mom or dad,
or doing your schoolwork,
or playing a game.

Siempre es bueno hacer las cosas

lo mejor que se puede . . .

como ayudar a

tu mamá o a tu papá,

o hacer la tarea,

o jugar a un juego.

And when you see
something small
that doesn't seem important,
remember that it is part
of something bigger.

Maybe it is something so great
that you can't even understand.

Y cuando veas algo pequeñito
que no parezca importante,
recuerda que es parte de algo mayor.

Quízas es algo de una grandeza tal
que ni siquiera se puede comprender.

This is my friend Daniela.
She reminds me that
all people are important
just because God made them.

Ésta es mi amiga Daniela.
Me ayuda a comprender que todos
somos importantes simplemente porque
Dios nos ha creado.

Sometimes smart is good.

A veces es bueno ser listo.

Loving other people just because God made them is always good.

Amar a otras personas sólo porque Dios las creó es siempre bueno.